Take off Time is a compilati
inspire the human spirit. Th
pain, and everything in betw
helping people become the b

would pour into others and not have enough energy for myself. These daily messages have been an inspiration to me, and I hope that you will be inspired as well.

The idea of a book came at a time I was contemplating moving back to my hometown in Ohio. It was 2014, and I was living in Bradenton, Florida. I was talking to a co-worker, Cody Hughes, about a title for a motivational book that I wanted to write, and he said, "Let me think about it." The next day he came to work and said, "Take Off Time." I asked why "Take Off Time" and he said, "Tim, it's time to let go of your past and fly to new levels. You take off, you land, and you take off again." Soon after, I decided on 31 topics I wanted to use as a platform to inspire others.

A year later, I put my actions to my words and moved back to my hometown Youngstown, Ohio, to help expand a youth program. For four years, 31 journal entries were compiled starting in March 2015 and completed in December 2019. Once completed, the journal was stored and waiting for the right time to be published. On April 13, 2020, the co-worker who gave me the title of the book passed away unexpectedly at the age of 32 in Bradenton, Florida. When I first heard the news, I instantly thought of him saying, "You take off, you land, you take off again." That day I pulled the journal out and began finalizing the rest of the entries to prepare for publishing. Publishing happened on Dec. 29, 2022, the same day my great nephew Dejuan Thomas III was born, and launched on Jan. 11, 2023.

I realize that words are powerful, and that it's my job to receive and distribute the words that are written. The reality of life is that many times you must encourage yourself. There is an old saying that goes, "If you stay ready, you don't have to get ready."

Tools to get the best out of the book:

-Find a quiet space to read.

-Ask God for clarity.

-Meditate.

-Apply principles to your life.

-Show gratitude in advance.

When you know your value, your choices are easy?

Day 1

Get Started

"The Way to Get Started Is To Quit Talking And Begin Doing." — _Walt Disney_

Welcome aboard leader. This message is for you. As you prepare to begin your day, it's important to know you are the change that you want to see in the world. The situation you're currently in may or may not be ideal, but it's your situation. You may be in an unstable home, in a bad relationship, hopeless, unemployed, incarcerated, depressed, or maybe even sick. If you're reading this, change for the better has begun. It's important to know that momentum is a powerful force, and once started, it's hard to stop; good or bad. The idea is to get momentum to work on your side. The best way for that to happen is to get started on the things you need to do. Once you get started, it will be much easier to keep going. Like a jet in full force when turbulence arises, momentum will carry you through the tough times. So, get started on whatever you need to do, even if it's baby steps. There are some things that you may have been putting off for years. Now is the time to approach your runway and activate the pilot within. Embrace the journey.

Day 2

Believe in Yourself

Believe you can and you're halfway there." – Theodore Roosevelt

To believe in yourself is to accept yourself; flaws and all. Once that foundation is established, you can build from there. Building that foundation takes some work, and that work begins in the mind. You're probably thinking, "Why the mind…?" You must start with the mind because it controls your perception of things, especially of yourself. Many men and women have changed the landscape of society because they believed in their talents and abilities. Your self-belief system is often shaped by your experiences in life and what someone has or hasn't said about who you are. Believing in yourself happens over time and through many failures. Not allowing those failures to define you is the key to having a strong belief system.

If this message finds you in a place of self-doubt, you may need to reprogram yourself and start with a blank canvas. If you're at a place where your belief system is strong, continue to fuel yourself with positive energy. The stronger your belief system gets, the more courage you will have to take on bigger challenges. Believing in yourself is contagious. Imagine how many people would impact the world for the betterment of society if they just believed in themselves.

Day 3

Trust the Process

"It's never too late to start walking in your purpose and living the life that is truly best for you. Outlast this season. Better is coming."
— **Germany Kent**

A process is a series of actions or steps taken to achieve an end. Anything of substance and value that was ever created went through a process. You were created through a process of nine months in your mother's womb. To create the lifestyle you want, it's going to take a similar process, not literally, but figuratively. The process that it's going to take to be the best version of yourself is a lifelong process. You must trust that the actions you're taking to be your best will reward you in time.

During the process, there will be times when all is going well, and times major setbacks may occur. You may be reading this message amid a setback. Don't allow this setback to kill the process. Accept it for what it is and figure out how to get back on track. A piece of coal goes through an immense amount of pressure, and an extensive amount of time before it becomes a diamond. The same goes for you. If you're going to be a contributor to society, you must trust that everything you're going through, and everything you're sacrificing is going to be beneficial for you. In the end, let the process to shape the diamond within take place. People will respect the process because they saw you accept the process.

Day 4

Patience

"Have patience with all things but first of all with yourself." —*Francis de Sales*.

There is a balancing act between patience and urgency, an act that is crucial for your success. We live in a microwave mentality society, where everything is expected to happen overnight. Patience is the capacity to accept or tolerate delay, trouble, or suffering without getting angry or upset. It is a tough pill to swallow, but once you're able to get it into your system, it will allow you to see the bigger picture of your situation. It also prepares you for your opportunity toward success. Patience allows you to deal with some very difficult people. It will allow the process to fully develop you. We reap what we sow, so you must be patient for the fruit to bear from your efforts. Nothing of value can be created immediately. There will be setbacks, discouragements, and delays. Patience helps keep everything in perspective, so be patient with yourself as you learn patience. The best is yet to come. Wait on it!

Day 5

Stay Ready

When you build in silence people don't know what to attack. - Anonymous

Many opportunities come across your path every day. Many of these opportunities can never be taken because you're not ready. Staying ready is a mindset you embrace so you are prepared for sudden life changes, whether good or bad. When good opportunities come your way, do not ignore them because another one is not promised. You may say that you're ready, but if your actions don't line up, you're fooling yourself. The world we live in has an abundance to give you, but you must position yourself to receive it. Sprinters prepare for months, even years, to be ready for a 12-second race in the Olympics. Winning the race is not contingent on the race, but on how one prepares. In the words of the famous race car driver Bobby Unser, "Success is where preparation and opportunity meet."

Day 6

Focus

Starve your distractions, feed your focus. - Anonymous

The need for you to focus is very important right now. There is so much to deal with, from work schedules, negative people, social media, friends, and even family. Focus on your focus, whether it be personal development, financial independence, graduating high school, or being a good parent. This information is critical to your success. A focused person doesn't allow the distractions of life to knock them off track. You are here now to make a difference in the world. People are depending on you to be focused. You being focused on your dreams and aspirations will change lives for generations to come, so focus on your gifts because that's what will open doors for you. Frailty comes from spreading things out, but there is power in concentrated focus. Focus on your goals my friend because most people want to waste your time.

Day 7

Choices and Consequences

Life is a matter of choices and every choice you make makes you. -John C. Maxwell

You had a choice today to pick up this book and read Day 7. Over time, if you continue to trust the process of becoming the best version of yourself, there will be positive consequences that follow. The choices you make today — knowingly and unknowingly — will shape your future. There is someone in your life that is giving you information and you choose to ignore them. The information they have may be what you need to help you accomplish your goals. Life-and-death choices are all around you, so choose wisely. There are people you are hanging around with that don't have the same goals. If you don't change your inner circle, your choices will have negative consequences that affect you. Choose today to be great, and everything else will fall into place.

Day 8

<u>Stay Humble</u>

"True humility is intelligent self-respect which keeps us from thinking too highly or too lowly of ourselves. -Anonymous

You came into this world with nothing, and when you leave you will take nothing with you. Never feel that you are above or beneath anyone. You live in a day and time that focuses on self-promotion. Social media makes it very easy to create a false perception of yourself. The quickest way to lose respect from people is to think you're better than them. When you let go of the need to impress others, that's when you become impressive. When you understand that your power comes from a higher source, there is no need to boast about yourself. Being humble is not a weakness, but a strength. Approach every situation with boldness and wait for the outcome with humility, knowing that everything will eventually work out for your good. Stay teachable, regardless of how much you know, or think you know, because there is always more to learn. Failure is inevitable as you strive to reach your goals. Humility helps cushion the fall, and it also helps you bounce back quickly.

Day 9

Effort and Attitude

The two things in life you are in total control over are your Attitude and your Effort. – Billy Cox

Life throws challenges at you every day, and it's up to you how you respond. Knowing that you are in control empowers you and empowers others around you. Instead of looking at a glass of water as half-empty, see it as half-full. When that happens, you are more optimistic about life. Your attitude and effort will take you to the next level in life if you stay positive. If you have a negative attitude and poor effort, you will be grounded and stuck in the rat race for survival or even worse. To move from surviving to thriving, you must choose how you react in every situation. Life may have dealt you a bad hand of cards or you may have been born with a silver spoon in your mouth. Whatever the case, you're still in control of the direction of your life. Don't allow circumstances to distract your attitude, and never give less than your best effort in all you do. When all is said and done, your quality of life depends on how you respond to life's challenges and the work you put into making a life of substance.

Day 10

Overcome Adversity

We fall, we break, we fail...But then we rise, we heal, we overcome. - Anonymous

Adversity presents itself in many forms: a prison sentence, loss of a job, bullying, unexpected pregnancy, or maybe even a death of a loved one. Adversity is inevitable. In life, when faced with it, you have a choice to overcome it or run from it. Running from it is very easy. Overcoming it is a lot tougher, but it makes you stronger in the long run. Overcoming adverse circumstances strengthens your self-esteem. In each challenge, there's an opportunity to grow and learn more about yourself. Some of the adverse circumstances you are in or have been in are because of poor decisions you've made. Don't repeat the cycle. However, there will be other adverse circumstances that are out of your control. Embrace the frustration, setback, or loss. Use it to inspire you and other people to overcome adversity. People don't care about the storms you have been through in life. They want to know if you made it out and what resources you used to do it. Some of the toughest times in life lead to some of the best moments in life. This book was inspired by someone who faced insurmountable adversities yet never gave up because people were depending on that person.

Day 11

Greatest Love of All

"Learn to love yourself enough to be happy in your own company, not needing to use anyone as an escape." —Samantha Camargo

Love is a word that is often used, and it arouses different emotions in different people. True love is not shown in words only but also in actions. You may be in a place where love is meaningless because the person who displayed it used it to take advantage of you. Don't allow that to defeat you. The greatest love of all is to love yourself. You can begin loving yourself by accepting who you are, despite your past. When you love yourself, you set your standards high, and don't trade your dignity for someone else to love you. You must realize that you're one of a kind. It's important to love yourself first because that's who you spend the most time with. Don't walk in the shadows of others. Remember: The greatest love of all is inside of you.

Day 12

Sacrifice

**Great achievement is usually born of great sacrifice and is never the result of selfishness.
-Napoleon Hill**

Sacrifice is something you give up, usually for the sake of a better version of yourself. For you to grow and reach your goals in life, it's going to take sacrifices. For you, that sacrifice may mean giving up sweets to lose weight or giving up parties for a period to focus on schoolwork, etc. Sacrifice can look different to everyone. Although different, the fact remains, you must give something up to get something in return. Suppose you want to start your own business, but your current job consumes a lot of your time. For that business to become a reality, you are going to have to burn the midnight oil and sacrifice sleep to make it happen. When the opportunity comes for you to start that business, you will have things in place. It's not going to be easy, but you must have the will to do it. Anything worth having is worth a sacrifice. Don't worry if you will be publicly recognized for your sacrifices. You know what you gave up making your dreams a reality. So, give. Give your time, your resources, and most importantly give your heart.

Day 13

Repetition

It's the repetition of affirmations that leads to belief." - Muhammad Ali

Repetition is the act of doing something repeatedly. Repetition is a powerful force, and you can dig a hole for yourself if self-destructive things are repeated. Repetition can also lift you out of a hole if positive actions are taken. You may be in a situation where your repetitive behaviors have you stuck and unsure what to do in your life. Now is the time to reverse the cycle and get unstuck and live your best life. It's said that insanity is doing the same thing repeatedly and expecting different results. However, it's almost always the people that are deemed insane who end up changing the world in the biggest ways. The repeated efforts of Orville and Wilbur Wright to fly gave us the first airplane. Whatever it is that you want to get unstuck from, you must find the right information so that you can implement the tactics correctly. It's not about practicing just to practice but practicing the right skills and techniques repeatedly that lead to success. Repetition builds stamina and allows you to bounce back quicker when you fall. It also builds self-confidence in your skills or talent. Repetition is your friend, and until you get to where you're trying to go, you're going to have to do the small things repeatedly well.

Day 14

Vision

Vision makes the unseen visible and the unknown possible. - Myles Munroe

Vision is the ability to see and plan the future with your imagination. Where you are right now doesn't mean it's where you'll always be. You must begin to look at life the way you want it to be. You must start seeing yourself as a homeowner, graduating college, being released from prison, as a millionaire, etc. Once you begin to see it, the law of attraction takes over. When I began writing this book, I envisioned it selling a million copies within its first five years of publication. I already know it will exceed that, but I had to shoot for a goal. The same goes for you. There's greatness that is bottled up within you. You must already see that greatness being uncapped. There may be a book, song, or business that is waiting to be released, but first, you must see the impact it is going to have on your life and others. The biggest adversary to vision is sight. It's very easy to lose your vision if your focus is only on where you are currently. Vision is the art of seeing the unseen, an art that many people choose not to develop. It's important to protect your vision. Some people are blind and can't see outside their comfort zone. Others just don't want your vision to come to fruition and will discourage or even sabotage your dreams. Stay away from those people. If you see it in your mind, work toward it. It may or may not come to fruition in your lifetime, but if you lay out a plan, someone will pick up where you left off and carry it on.

Day 15

The Enemy Within

The hardest battles are fought within yourself, against the person you used to be.

-David Caixeiro

Every day when you arise there is a voice in your head that gives you negative messages. Some call it the devil. I consider it the enemy within. The enemy within grows over time, and it feeds on the things you've been exposed to in your life. Maybe you've been abused, neglected, or rejected and the voice is louder than ever. To turn it off, you must first acknowledge its presence. The voice tells you things like 'you can't do it' or 'you're inadequate' or 'no one even cares. I'm here to tell you that those are all lies. You were created for a purpose, and your job is to find that purpose. While writing this book, I was bombarded with inner-voice messages that discouraged me, but I stood up to that voice and said I am somebody, I define success. I want to encourage you to do the same thing. The voice is a toothless lion that just wants to put fear in your heart. Fear is false evidence appearing real. You are going to fulfill the vision you have for your life, however, the enemy within will always be with you. Even though you hear it, that doesn't mean you have to believe what it says.

Day 16

Gratitude

"We often take for granted the very things that most deserve our gratitude." – Cynthia Ozick

Gratitude is the act of being thankful. You live in a world that constantly reminds you that you never have enough whether it be a new house, new car, new job, or a significant other. When you're thankful, you focus on the things and people you do have in your life, and it helps those things flourish. Get into the habit of telling people you love or who have helped you that you appreciate them. There may be someone who meant the world to you that is no longer living. You wish you could have let them know you appreciate the sacrifices they made for you, but it's too late to say it to them. Let your actions show they are appreciated by allowing the positive energy they invested in you to shine. Take a moment and reflect on your life. There are countless things you could be thankful for, from being able to walk to just having a bed to sleep in. You can't appreciate where you're going if you don't appreciate where you're at. I'm thankful that you took the time to read this message and take nothing for granted because tomorrow is not promised.

Day 17

Red Flags

Ignoring the red flags because you want to see the good in people will cost you later. - Anonymous

Red flags are signs that are given to warn you of possible danger. These signs pop up in relationships, businesses, and even everyday traffic. Ignoring red flags can be very costly even to the point of death. As you are learning how to love yourself more you will be able to recognize red flags. Many people have forfeited their greatness because they ignored a detour, stop or yield sign in the journey of life. The great news is that if you're reading this message, you can reclaim all that was taken. It all begins with you. Look at this message as a red flag warning you to pursue your dreams before it's too late. Separate yourself from people who don't value you or what you do. Most people will take it personally, but that's not your problem. Where you are trying to go, they're not ready yet and they may never be. Ignoring red flags is not easy because they come packaged with all types of people, places, and things. Move with confidence, approach cautiously, just don't get bitten by the same snake twice.

Day 18

Forgive

"**We must develop and maintain the capacity to forgive. He who is devoid of the power to forgive is devoid of the power to love.**"

- Martin Luther King Jr.

Anger, bitterness, fear, and resentment are all the symptoms of an unforgiving heart. Many people walk around in these mental and emotional prisons and are never free to live a purposeful life. Someone may have hurt you or will hurt you on this journey in life. The key is to not hold onto it. You may be saying I'm trying to let it go but it won't let go of me. I'm here to let you know that it's a lie from the enemy within. You are always bigger than your setback. Use the pain to inspire you to move forward. People are depending on you to forgive your past so that you can move forward. It's not that you forget what happened. You just can't let it define who you are. Forgiveness is not approving of what may have happened to you or trusting the person who hurt you. Instead, you are choosing not to be a victim anymore. Don't allow the mistakes of others to burden you and keep you from being the best version of yourself.

Day 19

Unity Over Self

Alone we can do so little; together we can do so much.

- Helen Keller

Unity is being together with someone or something. A unified group of people is a strength and can accomplish a lot. Becoming unified is the hard part. People naturally want to look out for their own self-interest, and by doing so they often miss out on great opportunities, opportunities that can serve your self-interest if you are willing to work with others. Unified groups are often divided by people who do not want to play their roles. On a team, no one is more important than the other. The issue that often arises is who is going to get the credit for the success. It's been said that you never know how far you can go if you don't care who gets the credit. Unity is about people working together to accomplish a bigger goal. You helping make someone else's dream become a reality can be the deciding factor of your own dreams coming true.

Day 20

Balance

"Life is about balance. Be kind, but don't let people abuse you. Trust, but don't be deceived. Be content, but never stop improving yourself."

— Zig Ziglar

Having a productive day requires getting rest. Getting rest will allow you to have a productive day. They balance each other out. Balance is essential in all aspects of life. This message may have found you in chaos, a bad relationship, financial distress, depression, or maybe even isolated from society. It's up to you to get it under control. You first must acknowledge life is unbalanced and identify the deficient areas. Once identified, see what needs to be increased and what needs to be decreased. What needs to be added? What needs to be cut off? Balance is a conscious process that changes every day. You must accept what you can't change and change the things you can. Never take on more than you can handle, and let go of that which you cannot handle. Remember: Life is a constant battle of letting go and hanging on.

Day 21

Win the Day

"If you want to conquer the anxiety of life, live in the moment, live in the breath."
— Amit Ray

There are only so many things you can control, and for those you can control, you must do so. As you continue this journey in life, it's going to be important that you take it in stride. Each day comes with new challenges — a lot of them unexpected. As you address those challenges, don't see them as obstacles but opportunities, opportunities to grow, because if it doesn't kill you it's going to make you stronger. But when it is time to go you know you gave a valiant effort. Approach each day with gratitude (Remember Day 16). Winning the day is a conscious effort. Today, let someone you love know they are loved. Spend some quality time with yourself, meditating on the goodness of life. You may not be in the situation you want to be in but if you're at least reading this message you're doing a little better than others. So, appreciate where you're at, look forward to where you're going, and stay humbled by your past.

Day 22

Set them and reach them

"Focused, hard work is the real key to success. Keep your eyes on the goal, and just keep taking the next step towards completing it.

- **Anonymous**

There are many things you want to do, but they can't all be done at once. You must step back and prioritize what is important. Your goals must be set to make sure you follow through. Goals keep you on track, whether it be financial goals, relationship goals, or career goals. When writing these inspired messages, I had to set goals to ensure this book was created. Here's a flow chart of how this book was produced.

1st: What type of book do I want to create — Daily Inspiration

2nd: Book Title — "Take Off Time"

3rd: Subject Matter — 31 topics that apply to everyday life

4th: Quotes — 31 unique quotes that galvanize each message

5th: Writing Content — 31 Inspired messages from T.A Frost's life journey.

6th: Type and Edit — (Grammarly.com)

7th: Develop Cover

8th: Send to Publisher (kdp.amazon.com)

9th: Book Launch

Because I set small goals, and reached them, you can read this book. You could apply the same steps to whatever you're working on. Many men and women have never reached their full potential because they didn't set goals and reached them. You don't want to be one of those people!

Day 23

<u>Create your terms</u>

The only person who is going to give you security and the life you want is you.

-Anonymous

To have a fulfilling life, you must create the terms. When you set goals, it's easy to identify the conditions needed to reach those goals. Terms are conditions one subjects himself or herself to fulfill a commitment. Often people lower their moral standards to fulfill terms. You may be in financial chaos right now and see no end to the debt you have incurred. You must first evaluate your income versus your spending. You can then see where you can cut back. You also need to figure out how you can create more income streams. To have the life you deserve, it's going to take a lot of blood, sweat, and tears. It will be worth it in creating your terms to never sacrifice your dignity. Don't compromise your integrity for money, power, or respect. Write your terms down. Conceive them. Believe them, then achieve them.

Day 24

Lifelong learner

"Anyone who stops learning is old, whether at twenty or eighty. Anyone who keeps learning stays young.

-Anonymous

To learn is to acquire knowledge or a skill or something by studying, experiencing, or being taught. The first thing you must learn is about yourself. Learn your strengths and weakness, what triggers you, what's fulfilling, and what's not. Once you have a strong sense of self, you can retain information from outside sources. Life is always changing, so you must learn to adapt. Adapting doesn't mean you compromise good for evil. It means you adjust your approach to how you handle a situation. Surround yourself with people who are smarter than you. If you're the smartest in the group, you become complacent, and you're preparing for a major setback. Learn from the mistakes you made and learn from other people's mistakes. Learn from other people's success as well and find out what they did to get the results they wanted. Never think you know it all. No one wants to be around a person with all the answers. Don't learn just how to store information but learn how to apply information, also.

Day 25

Invest in yourself

Change equals self-improvement. Push yourself to places you haven't been before."

—Pat Summitt

Your value rises when you invest in yourself. You become a talent-plus person. A talent-plus person has enhanced their natural talent by investing in themselves. You invest in yourself when you take time to read literature such as this. You invest in yourself when you save up your money to get your business started. Before you can invest in others you first have to have something of value to give — whether it be emotional, financial, or educational. Your most valuable resource is your mind. Use it wisely. As you invest in yourself, be patient. It may take some time to see a turnaround in your investment. You are worthy to be invested in, so don't second guess yourself. At the end of the day, you know what it took to make your dreams a reality.

Day 26

Know when to walk away

Accept yourself, love yourself, and keep moving forward. If you want to fly, you have to give up what weighs you down.
– Roy T. Bennett.

You're going to encounter many different people, places, and things on life's journey. They all may serve you respectively for a period. Regardless of the people, places, or things, don't allow them to take you off track from reaching your goals. God created us as social beings. There are some people that will be hard to leave. A lot of times the ones holding you back are family and friends, often not intentionally, but out of fear of losing you. You must know when to keep them and when to let them go. You can't take everyone with you. As it pertains to places, some places you attend or hang out are not helping you get to where you're trying to go. You may have to re-evaluate and find a positive alternative to the places that are holding you back. Some things can be addictive. They lure you in with their pleasures and then mentally enslave you. Things can be money, drugs, or even positions of power. Never sell out to acquire material things. If forced to decide between compromising your integrity, walk away!

Day 27

Relay Race

A life is not important except in the impact it has on other lives.

Jackie Robinson

A desire for a successful life is not a sprint or a marathon but a relay. You must understand that all the information you obtain is not meant for you to take to the grave. It's meant to be shared with the next generation. In a relay, the runner runs with the baton and once they run their legs, they pass it on to the next runner. The same goes in life. You're only here for a season and during your season you must upload all you can and then download your information to someone else before your season ends. Since you don't know when your season will end, you must act with a sense of urgency. Don't wait until you're on your deathbed to pass the baton. As you build your legacy, it's important to prepare a successor, someone who will carry on what you started. That may be a son, brother, friend, or business partner. Many men and women lie in their caskets with a baton in their hands because they were too selfish to hand them off. What you do for yourself dies with you. What you do for others remains and is immortal. (Robert Pike)

Day 28

Passion

No alarm clock needed; my passion wakes me up.

-Eric Thomas

Passion is an uncontrollable emotion. When you become passionate you become unstoppable. The key is directing that energy toward the right thing. As it pertains to the good in life, you must search for what motivates you. For me, I'm passionate about empowering, enlightening, and emancipating the fatherless and oppressed so that they can become the best version of themselves. This passion was not discovered overnight. It took time, achievement, and failure to awaken me to what I'm passionate about. Take a moment and think about what you love doing for free. If there is something with which you identify, there lies your passion. If you're still searching, ask people close to you what they feel you're good at. You don't have to rely solely on their opinion, but it gives you some direction. Remember: In finding your passion you must believe it exists, be open-minded and seek opportunities that are appealing to you. Your passion will lead you to your purpose. Your purpose is what you were born to do. Passion and purpose work hand in hand, so live each day like it is your last.

Day 29

Victim or Victor

"The habits that govern our lives determines if we will be victors or victims."
— **Benjamin Suulola**

Society has a way of making you feel like a victim. Feelings of helplessness, entitlement, and aggression are signs of a victim-minded person. The reality of life is that things are going to happen that are out of our control. It's not what happens but how you respond to what happens. John Maxwell, a well-known author and pastor, said life is 10 percent what happens to you at 90 percent how you respond. Don't see your challenges as something happening to you, but as something happening for you to build your endurance in life. It's important to learn from other's mistakes and not to make the same ones. A victor accepts that they can't change everything. But an overcomer works at changing the things they can. A victor, when it's all said and done, has no regrets and has made a positive contribution to society. Hopefully, this message reaches you with a victor mentality. If not, be encouraged and acknowledge where you are and seek the right support. Remember your best days are ahead of you!

Day 30

Faith is the Key

My faith helps me understand that circumstances don't dictate my happiness, my inner peace.

-Denzel Washington

The most important ingredient to making your dreams come to reality is faith. Faith is believing that the vision God gave you will come to pass. The frustrating thing is that sometimes you may not live to see your vision come to full bloom. But you must act accordingly as if you already see it and establish a plan to be followed. Faith is a universal power that attracts things to you as you work toward them. Your faith will be tested daily. Don't give up, and don't give in. When doubt creeps in, affirm to yourself I believe even when the storms of life are raging, I have faith that this too shall pass.

Day 31

Finish Strong

Starting strong is good, finishing strong is epic.
-Anonymous

Starting something in life is easy. The challenge is finishing whatever you start. Even when you try something new for the first time, give yourself the time to adjust to new environments and situations. If it's not going against your morals and values, see it all the way through. The butterfly starts as a caterpillar and overcomes many challenges before it reaches its beautiful stage of fluttering around, beautifying the world. You may be going through a tough time right now, but remember everything happens for a reason. Ask God to give you the strength to complete your temporary journey here on earth. Keep your commitment to your commitment. People are depending on you to finish strong.

I dedicate this book to my "Childhood Friends" who took off much earlier than expected, unfortunately, due to gun violence. You are loved, missed, and honored every single day. You did not die in vain!

25% of the proceeds of this book will go to the launching and sustaining of Replay Preserve Homes. These are loving residential homes for children who are returning to society from being incarcerated and would prefer a positive environment over the toxic one that contributed to their problems.

WWW.REPLAYOUTREACH.ORG

Replay Outreach is a non-profit organization established in Bradenton, Florida, in 2012. We encourage at-risk teens to uncover their purpose in life, learn to manage their behavior, and gain the skills and attitudes that will lead to success.

Special Thanks:

Leslie Kitchen

Candys Mayo

Ernest Brown Jr.

Contact:

Merchandise/Speaking Engagements/Coaching

WWW.THECHANGEFACTORY.ORG

Notes:

Change Factory Production

"I'm not saying I'm going to Change the World, but I guarantee I'll SPARK the MIND that will."

-Tupac Amaru Shakur-

Made in the USA
Middletown, DE
08 May 2025